ORIGAMI HEART

written AND Illustrated

by BINNY

Hodder
Children's
Books

In a burrow in the sky, amongst the clouds of a metropolis, lives a lovely NEAT rabbit boy named KABUKI.

KABUKI likes everything to be just so.

KABUKI is alone in this bustling city, but today his friend YOKO is coming to visit.

In the morning he dresses carefully for his guest. First indigo trousers, then glasses, a BOW TIE and a satchel.

KABUKI goes to the market.

He seeks PERFECTION in vegetables.

He searches for <u>excellence</u> in snow pea tea.

He looks for symmetry in flowers.

KABUKI is VERY particular indeed.

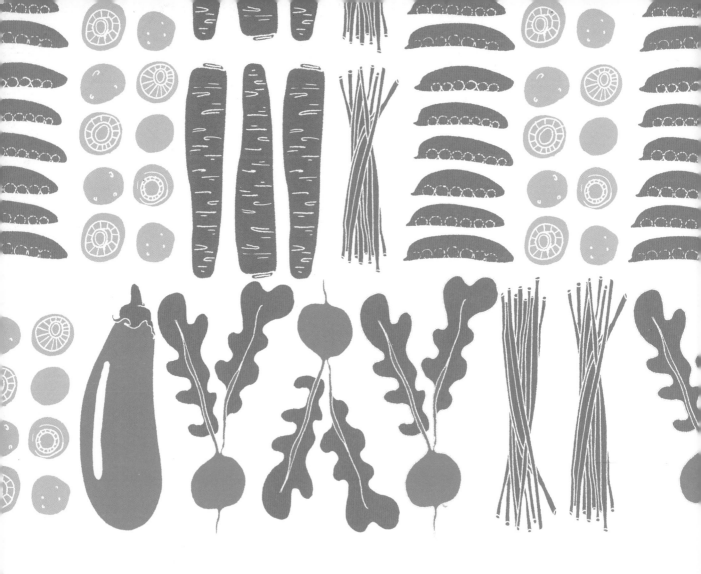

When he gets home, KABUKI lines up all his __PERFECT__ new items in neat rows on the kitchen bench.

He dices the carrots and radishes
into exact HEART shapes.

The table is set for <u>Two</u>.

He TWEAKS his long whiskers,
perches on a cushion and
WAITS for Yoko.

And waits

...and <u>WAITS</u>.

tippetty tap
tippetty tap

His ears stand STRAIGHT.

He fluffs his tail.

But it's not YOKO. It is the postman..

KABUKI reads the note from YOKO.

A single tear rolls down his
face and SPLASHES onto the floor.

He takes a deep breath, unpins his heart patch
from his chest and SMOOTHS it out
flat on the table in front of him.

KABUKI ever so carefully folds his heart into a beautiful, crisp PAPER PLANE.

He STANDS UP, opens the window and THROWS the plane out to the bustling city below.

Down in the city, a DAINTY bunny is ON her way HOME. Out of the corner of her eye she sees something FLUTTER from the sky. She catches it.

She CATCHES KABUKI'S heart.

- THE END -

How to MAKe an Origami HeaRT

You will need:
• A square piece of coloured paper

Take your piece of coloured paper
and fold it using the instructions
opposite. Each time you fold the
paper, run your finger or thumb
along the folded edge to flatten it.
This will make the finished heart
look neat.

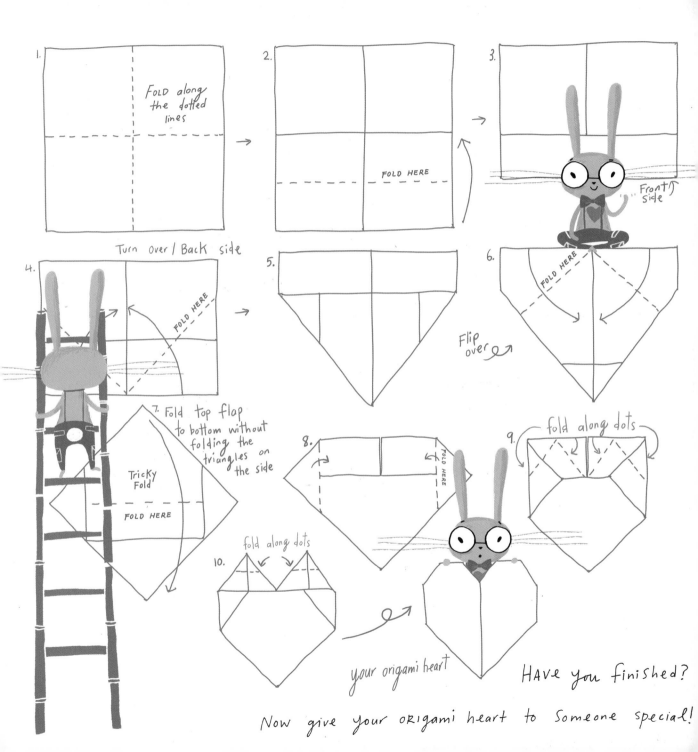

1. FOLD along the dotted lines

2. FOLD HERE

3. Front Side

Turn over / Back side

4. FOLD HERE

5.

6. FOLD HERE

Flip over

7. Fold top flap to bottom without folding the triangles on the side

Tricky Fold

FOLD HERE

8. FOLD HERE

9. fold along dots

10. fold along dots

your origami heart

HAVE you finished?

Now give your origami heart to someone special!

How to Make an Origami Rabbit

You will need:
- A square piece of white or coloured paper
- Coloured pens or pencils

Take your piece of coloured paper and fold it using the instructions below.

1.

FOLD HERE

2.

FOLD HERE

3.

FOLD HERE

4.

FOLD along
the dotted
lines

5.

FLIP
over

6.

FOLD backwards along
the dotted line
but don't fold
back ears

7.

FOLD backwards along
the dotted
line

8.

Once your rabbit is ready
give it eyes, a nose, a mouth
— and some long whiskers,
like KABUKI!

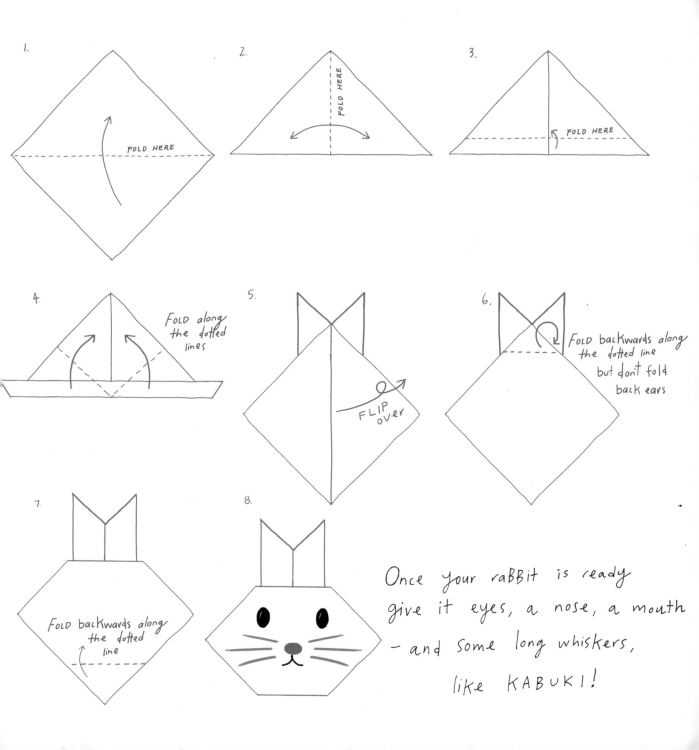

How to Make an Origami Plane

You will need:
- A square piece of coloured paper
- A pen or pencil

Write a note to a friend or family member on your piece of paper. You could write a poem, or tell a secret — or just tell them how you feel. Now follow the instruction to turn it into a paper plane.

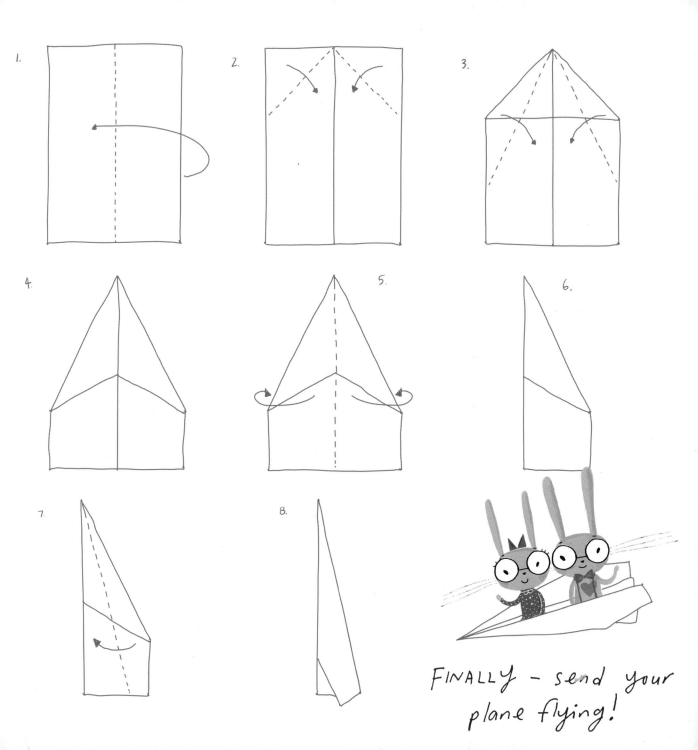

1.

2.

3.

4.

5.

6.

7.

8.

FINALLY — send your plane flying!

I have always been inspired by the culture of Japan. Many Japanese traditions go back thousands of years — the art of origami is over 4000 years old. Origami is still popular with people (and rabbits!) of all ages.

Did you notice that Kabuki lives high up in the sky? Japan is made up of islands and its area is very small. Lots of people live there, so buildings have to be tall to be able to fit everyone in. It's useful to be neat when you live in a small space, like Kabuki does!

Kabuki prepares his food neatly too. Sushi is a favourite Japanese dish: carefully arranged parcels of raw fish, vegetables and rice. It's delicious — especially if it's served with Kabuki's snow pea tea!

I hope you've enjoyed Kabuki's story. Don't forget to give your origami heart to someone special!

BINNY